Red Fox

my favorite animal

Published in the United States of America by Cherry Lake Publishing
Ann Arbor, Michigan
www.cherrylakepublishing.com

Reading Adviser: Marla Conn MS, Ed., Literacy specialist, Read-Ability, Inc.
Book Design: Jennifer Wahi
Illustrator: Jeff Bane

Photo Credits: © Marcin Perkowski / Shutterstock.com, 5; © Josef Pittner / Shutterstock.com, 7; © Alexey Osokin / Shutterstock.com, 9; © Paul Reeves Photography / Shutterstock.com, 11; © leungchopan / Shutterstock.com, 13; © DextairPhotography / Shutterstock.com, 15; © Ray Hennessy / Shutterstock.com, 17; © David Havel / Shutterstock.com, 19; © Menno Schaefer / Shutterstock.com, 21; © Geoffrey Kuchera / Shutterstock.com, 23; © Ozerina Anna 2-3, 24; Cover, 1, 8, 12, 20, Jeff Bane

Library of Congress Cataloging-in-Publication Data has been filed and is available at catalog.loc.gov

Printed in the United States of America
Corporate Graphics

table of contents

About the author: Dr. Virginia Loh-Hagan is an author, university professor, former classroom teacher, and curriculum designer. She thinks her dogs are tricky like foxes. She lives in San Diego with her very tall husband and very naughty dogs. To learn more about her, visit www.virginialoh.com.

About the illustrator: Jeff Bane and his two business partners own a studio along the American River in Folsom, California, home of the 1849 Gold Rush. When Jeff's not sketching or illustrating for clients, he's either swimming or kayaking in the river to relax.

looks

Red foxes have red fur. Some have gray patches. They have a white chest. They have black legs and ears.

Their tail has a white tip. The tail is bushy. It is thick. It helps red foxes keep their balance. It helps them stay warm.

Red foxes weigh about 30 pounds (14 kilograms). They have a long body and tail. They have a long **snout**. They have short legs.

home

Red foxes live in the northern part of the world. Most live in the **wild**. They like forests, grasslands, and mountains. Some live on farms. Some live in cities.

Some red foxes like to sleep in the open. Some sleep in **dens**. They wrap their tail around them. This keeps them warm.

food

Red foxes eat meat. They eat small animals like mice, rabbits, and birds. They also eat eggs and fruit.

Red foxes are good at finding food. They hunt alone. They follow **prey**. Then they **pounce**.

Red foxes are quick and **agile**. They jump high. They swim well. They hear well. They can hear prey underground. They dig them out.

Red foxes **communicate** with each other. They move their ears. They move their tails. They **arch** their backs.

Females build dens. They dig tunnels. They have **kits**. Males bring them food. Red foxes live in family groups.

glossary & index

glossary

agile (AJ-il) able to move quickly and easily

arch (AHRCH) to form a round shape

communicate (kuh-MYOO-nih-kate) to use actions that let someone else know what you're thinking

dens (DENZ) animal homes like caves or holes in the ground

kits (KITS) baby foxes

pounce (POUNS) to jump forward and grab something suddenly

prey (PRAY) animals hunted for food

snout (SNOUT) long front part of an animal's head where the nose and mouth are

wild (WILDE) natural places like the woods, mountains, and fields

index